B is for the special way you *brighten* up each day.

C
is for your *courage.*
You don't fear
what to do.

This book was made especially for:

AUSTIN

Dear Austin,

Words cannot express how special you are. But, here are twenty-six that try! Each one so perfectly describes you. You are all of these wonderful qualities— and so much more.

Love,

_____

A is for *amazing*.
That's Austin
in every way!

D

is for your *daring.*
You always
carry through.

E is for your *energy*, so vibrant and so bright!

F is for the *fun* you bring to all both day and night.

G describes your future. Oh, the places you will *go!*

H is for the *heights* you'll climb and successes you will know.

I's *imagination* and the power of your dreams.

J is for the *joy* you bring, your shining face that beams.

K

is for your *kindness*, shown to big and small.

L is for the *love*
you freely share
with one and all.

M is for your *music*, the song of your own heart.

N is meant for *never*, for we'll never, *ever* part.

O means there is *one* you—there never will be two!

P

is meant for *perfect*—it's you just being you.

Q is all the *qualities* I notice every time.

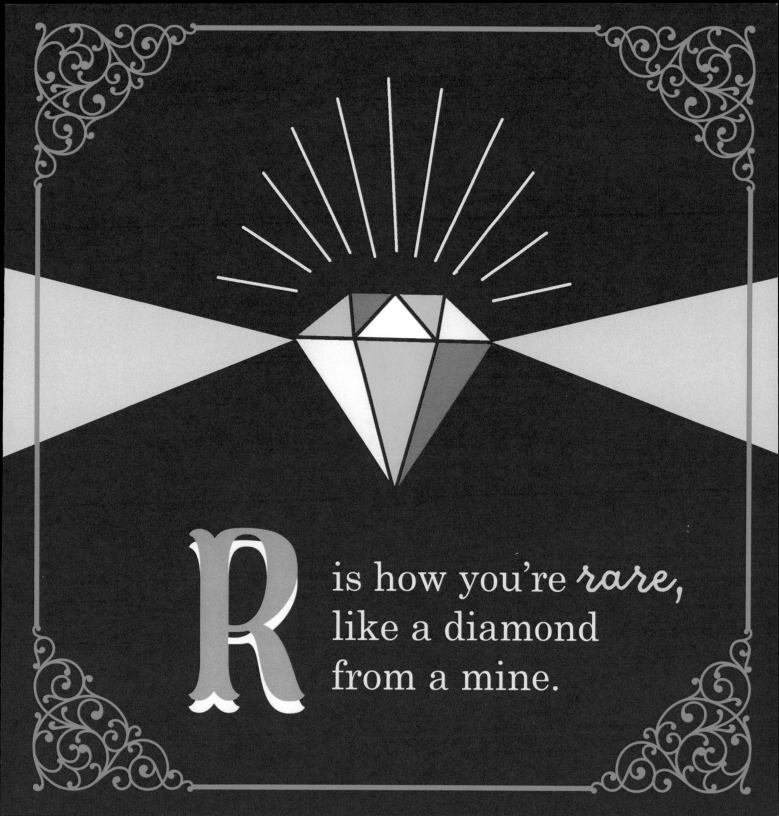

R is how you're *rare*, like a diamond from a mine.

S is meant for *super*,
for you have pow'r
to soar!

T is for the *talents* that you have (and so much more!)

U is for *unique*
in every bold sense
of the word.

V is for your *voice*. Don't be afraid that you'll be heard!

W is for *wild*.
Always live and
gallop free!

X
is xceptional,
xtraordinarily!

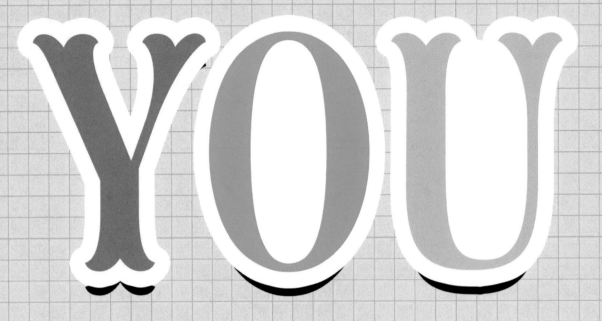

YOU

Y is meant for *you*,
the only one
there'll ever be.

But day is done, and you
must sleep, so

Z

now stands for
zzzzzzzzzzz...

Li'l Llama
CUSTOM KIDS BOOKS

Cover and book design by David Miles

Visual credits: bear with umbrella, bear with ice cream, giraffe on bicycle, bear on bicycle, bear on unicycle, dog on scooter (StudioLondon/Shutterstock.com); boat (NadineVeresk/Shutterstock.com); sloth (jsabirova/Shutterstock.com); wave pattern (Vecteezy.com); dancing horse, llama, super dog, zebra, birds, dinosaur, deer, cat and dog, cat and bird, unicorn (lena_nikolaeva/Shutterstock.com); tree branches (Ardea-studio/Shutterstock.com); cloud pattern (love pattern/Shutterstock.com); bird tree branch (PinkPueblo/Shutterstock.com); mouse (Nadezda Barkova/Shutterstock.com); cooking items, space elements (Beskova Ekaterina/Shutterstock.com); diamond (Olga_Angelloz/Shutterstock.com); leaf pattern (Mangata/Shutterstock.com); singing cat, astronaut mouse, monkey sailor (Maria Skrigan/Shutterstock.com); rabbits (Natasha_Chetkova/Shutterstock.com); village (ussr/Shutterstock.com); radial burst (HPLTW/Shutterstock.com); goat (Tartila/Shutterstock.com); mountains (LoveZ/Shutterstock.com); animals in hot air balloon (Maria Starus/Shutterstock.com); flowers (mejorana/Shutterstock.com); rainbow (fruestig/Shutterstock.com); sun (Nikolaeva/Shutterstock.com); spine pattern (Curly Pat/Shutterstock.com); page borders (Giraphics/Shutterstock.com); clouds (Marina_Che/Shutterstock.com); large rainbow (Peter Hermes Furian/Shutterstock.com); graph paper background (Vector Plus Image/Shutterstock.com).

Made in the USA
Coppell, TX
20 June 2022

79045046R00019